Jumping Off Library Shelves

A BOOK OF POEMS

SELECTED BY LEE BENNETT HOPKINS

ILLUSTRATED BY JANE MANNING

WORDSONG

AN IMPRINT OF HIGHLIGHTS

Honesdale, Pennsylvania

Contents

Breakfast Between the Shelves

REBECCA KAI DOTLICH

Morning pours spoons of sun
through tall windows, rests along
a reading chair, a copper rail;
hovers over crumbs, small supper scraps
left by those who opened books
last night, to live in story.

Mice scamper
between shelves,
pass poems
like platters of cheese;

Please read this about Owl!
And this about Giant!

They find words
sprinkled like cracker salt
on all those pages
where genius weaves letters
into magic; beckons new readers:

Look! This is the book for you.

Morning pours spoons of sun.

Refuge

NIKKI GRIMES

My library comes into view.
Almost there!
I sprint the last few yards,
charge up the stone steps, breathless,
and push through the double doors,
smiling at the sweet kingdom of story
inviting me in
to rest, to explore—
to dream.

At the Library

MICHELE KRUEGER

I want to lock
the library door,
barricade it
ceiling to floor.

I've found a treasure,
a literal pleasure,

a book
I've not read
before.

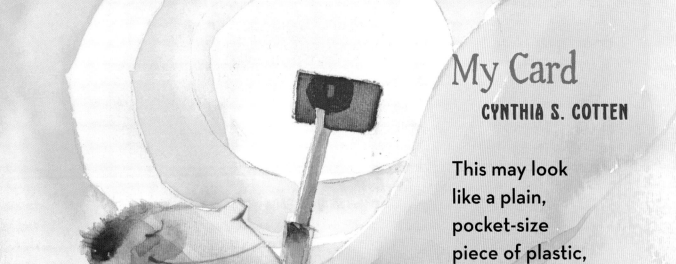

My Card
CYNTHIA S. COTTEN

This may look
like a plain,
pocket-size
piece of plastic,
but it's really
a super-card.

More powerful than
the smartest phone,
more powerful than
a TV remote,
more powerful than
a hundred apps.

My library card
unlocks the world
and more
with a single
scan.

Enchantment

JANE YOLEN

Stack by stack,
shelf by shelf,
I pick out books
all by myself.

Page by page,
line by line,
word by word,
I make books mine.

With a wave of a card
like a wizard's right hand—
and an alphabet-alchemy,
life
is
just
grand.

Internet Explorer

J. PATRICK LEWIS

On your desk sits the vagabond tutor;
SS *Library* serves as your ship.
If you wander the world by computer,
How far you can travel by chip.

Once your teacher has given you orders,
You're the captain, the cook, and the crew.
You can see from on deck or in quarters
What two-hand navigation can do.

For search engines, this key is your starter.
SS *Library* hums. It's a cinch!
By exploring the world, how much smarter
You are without moving an inch.

I'd Like a Story

X. J. KENNEDY

I'd like a story of
  Ghosts on gusty nights,
    Wild island ponies galloping
      With manes that wave like kites,
        A book that knows the lowdown
          On what to feed giraffes,
            A book of nutty nonsense
              That's nothing much—just laughs—

A book to read to find out
  How basketball stars shoot,
    Why dinosaurs all died out,
      What do computers compute,
        Which sail a mizzen sail is,
          Can Martians really be,
            How heavy a blue whale is,
              Weighed side by side with me—

A book to curl in bed with,
  To browse in by a brook—
    Anytime!
      Anyplace!
I'd like a book!

Librarian

JOAN BRANSFIELD GRAHAM

How did you
know?

Can you read
my mind?

How do you
always find
the perfect
book?

You get that
look
in your eyes
and there
it is . . .

another
surprise
to savor.

You watched,
listened,
sized me up
from the start:

you've been a
friend,
you
read
my
heart.

Storyteller

(For Augusta Baker)

LEE BENNETT HOPKINS

As she speaks
words
leap from pages—

there are
friends like
frog and toad—

I walk
down a
yellow brick road.

Worlds of paper
disappear—

only
Miss Augusta
and I
are here
in a room
filled with magic
story
rhyme.

And as her voice
reaches
the highest
rafter—

I believe in

once-upon-a-time,

I believe in

happily ever after.

Dictionary Dare

DEBORAH RUDDELL

Lift my chunky syllables,
my pounds of nouns,
my burly verbs.

Raise me above your head,
feel the quiet weight
of words.

The Poetry Section

ALICE SCHERTLE

The poetry section
was perfectly quiet.
I chose a collection,
decided I'd try it,

just thumb through the pages,
take a quick look
to see if I liked it.
I opened the book.

It reached out and *grabbed* me!
That poetry sound
set my heart singing,
spun me around

like a million bells ringing,
a hundred-piece band—
those poems made music
right there in my hand.

The library rocked
from the roof to the floor.

Perfectly quiet?
Well not anymore!

Reading with Riley

KRISTINE O'CONNELL GEORGE

So peaceful
in our corner of the library,
big ol' Riley, my reading buddy—
head on his paws,
warm, soft pillow—

all ears, all listen,
as we snuggle deeper
into story.

Warm

ANN WHITFORD PAUL

Winter winds howl, yet
we stay warm, wrapped in cozy
pages of our book.

Book Pillows

AMY LUDWIG VANDERWATER

With my head on a book
I dream of a place
where a pig loves a spider.

I dream of a face
high in a tower
with ropes of hair falling.

When books become pillows
stories come calling—

Wild things on a rumpus!
Fat evil kings!
Boy wizards, girl witches!
Horses with wings!

Stars shine on shelves
as I rest my full head
on book
after book
each a dream
I once read.

Midnight in a Library

REBECCA KAI DOTLICH

Night falls outside a window;
a mouse family huddles in a corner
shadowed by shelves—

hush! a squeak, a word,
a fable found,
                read,
                        heard.

A tiny crowd listens
to a mystery,
to "Once upon a time . . ."

            echoing there—

whiskers, tails twitch,
there's magic in the air;

a mouse family huddles in a corner
shadowed by shelves—

night falls
            outside
                    a
                        window.

Text copyright © 2015 by Lee Bennett Hopkins
Illustrations copyright © 2015 by Jane Manning
All rights reserved
For information about permission to reproduce selections
from this book, please contact permissions@highlights.com.

WordSong
An Imprint of Highlights
815 Church Street
Honesdale, Pennsylvania 18431
Printed in China

ISBN: 978-1-59078-924-7
Library of Congress Control Number: 2014958686

First edition
Design by Barbara Grzeslo
Production by Sue Cole
The text of this book is set in Neutraface.
The paintings are done in Winsor Newton gouache and
pencil on Lanaquarelle paper.

10 9 8 7 6 5 4 3 2 1

Thanks are due to the following for use of works in this collection:

Curtis Brown, Ltd. for "Breakfast Between the Shelves" and
"Midnight in a Library" by Rebecca Kai Dotlich, copyright © 2015
by Rebecca Kai Dotlich; "Refuge" by Nikki Grimes, copyright
© 2015 by Nikki Grimes; "Storyteller (For Augusta Baker)" by
Lee Bennett Hopkins, copyright © 2015 by Lee Bennett Hopkins;
"Book Pillows" by Amy Ludwig VanDerwater, copyright © 2015 by
Amy Ludwig VanDerwater; and "Enchantment" by Jane Yolen,
copyright © 2015 by Jane Yolen. All printed by permission of
Curtis Brown, Ltd.

All other works are used by permission of the respective poets,
who control all rights: Cynthia S. Cotten for "My Card"; Kristine
O'Connell George for "Reading with Riley"; Joan Bransfield
Graham for "Librarian"; X. J. Kennedy for "I'd Like a Story";
Michele Krueger for "At the Library"; J. Patrick Lewis for "Internet
Explorer"; Ann Whitford Paul for "Warm"; Deborah Ruddell for
"Dictionary Dare"; Alice Schertle for "The Poetry Section."

To Susan LosHuertos—
"This is the book for you."

—LBH

For Tatiana, with love

—JM